The Prayer of a Righteous Man

The Story of Daniel & The Lions' Den

Shepherd's Tales™

"Bringing God's Word to *LIFE*!"

Retold by Julie A. Voudrie

Illustrated by Bryant Owens

The Story of Daniel & The Lion's Den: The Prayer of a Righteous Man
Retold by: Julie A. Voudrie
Illustrations: Bryant Owens
Sidebars: Dr. Lee Magness & Julie Voudrie
Managing Editor: Jeffrey D. Voudrie
Published by Shepherd's Press™
a part of Shepherd's Tales™
Copyright © 1995 Shepherd's Tales™

ISBN 1-886858-24-1
UPC 789297005027

Printed in USA

For information:
Shepherd's Tales
P.O. Box 1911
Johnson City, TN 37605-1911
1-800-621-8904

From the owners of Shepherd's Tales™ :

Welcome to the Shepherd's Tales™ family! We hope this book brings you many hours of enjoyment. Shepherd's Tales™ is a family-owned company with a desire to bring God's Word to life in a way that ignites the imagination, while more importantly, illuminating the spirit.

Although these books are designed as companions to Shepherd's Tales™ Bible Story Cassettes, we couldn't possibly include thirty minutes of dialogue into 32 pages! For younger children, these books will fuel their imagination as they listen to the story on tape. For older children, the additional information found in the side-bars will give them a more in-depth look into spiritual truths as well as the history of biblical times. Scripture references included in the side-bars will also encourage further Bible study.

When combined with reading the biblical text, the exciting listening experience of Shepherd's Tales™ Bible Story Cassettes and the vivid illustrations of Shepherd's Tales™ Bible Storybook Companions will create a deeper understanding of who God is and how He works in the lives of His people. We hope you enjoy your journey into the incredible lives of God's people and pray that His word will be brought to life in the heart of your family.

Jeff and Julie Voudrie

This story is about a proud king, his jealous rulers and a humble man of God named Daniel.

Long ago, the people of Israel were taken as slaves to a faraway place called Babylon. One of these Israelite slaves was a man of God named Daniel. Daniel, who was by now over 80 years old, had been brought to Babylon when he was just a youth. He had served as advisor to the kings of Babylon through the years.

Daniel was known to be a very righteous man. Out of love for God, Daniel prayed to Him, in front of his open window, three times every day. God had given Daniel great abilities and wisdom because Daniel trusted in Him.

One day King Darius, the king of Babylon, issued a law about prayer. He ordered his messengers to proclaim the following decree throughout the land:

"Listen all people to the word of the mighty and powerful King Darius of Babylon! For the next thirty days, no one is to pray to any other god or man except to the King. Anyone who does pray to anyone else will be thrown into the lions' den."

The people of Babylon wondered why the King had issued such a law. What they didn't know was that a few days earlier some very strange events had taken place. Soon the King would regret that he had ever made his law on prayer.

Daniel found himself in a powerful city with a long history. It lay where the Tower of "Babel" had been (Gen. 11:9), in modern Iraq, where the Desert Storm War was fought. But the city came to dominate much of what we call the Middle East.

One of Babylon's early leaders was Hammurapi, who made the city a trading center and capital of a vast empire. His famous law codes are among the oldest legal documents, but he also sponsored great advances in literature, mathematics, and astronomy. After centuries of Assyrian domination, Babylon rose to new heights of power and prosperity under Nebuchadnezzar, one of the kings in Daniel, a great builder of buildings and empires.

Babylonians not only worshiped their emperor, but gods and goddesses who they believed ruled various parts of the world and aspects of life. Marduk was their sky-god, Tiamat was an evil sea-goddess, and Ishtar was a goddess of life.

Daniel's faithfulness to God and strength of character were lived out in the midst of paganism and worldly power. Later, Christians used "Babylon" as the symbol of persecution under which they, like Daniel, remained faithful and strong in the Lord. —Dr. Lee Magness (see Romans 12:2,& Revelation 18)

A few days before the King issued his strange law, he summoned together all his rulers, called satraps, and his three advisors, including Daniel. He told them to come to his palace throne room to hear an important announcement.

"As you know, for some time now I've been considering a change in the governing of my kingdom," explained King Darius." I have decided to place one of my most trusted advisors in charge of the whole realm. I have complete trust in him to faithfully carry out his new duties. The man I have chosen is none other than Daniel."

The men were angry. They were not happy with the King's choice.

"To prepare for his new duties," the King continued, "Daniel will be away tomorrow, inspecting some of my farmlands and canals." The King rose from his throne. He motioned for Daniel to join him as the other men left the room.

The satraps and other advisors began to grumble and complain among themselves. They were jealous of Daniel's abilities and of his influence with the King. As they left the palace, they became furious that the King would place Daniel in charge of them and the kingdom. A few of the more powerful satraps began to plot a way to get rid of Daniel.

"What does King Darius think he's doing —putting that slave in charge of us?" exclaimed one of the older satraps. "To give that position to a foreigner — it's just not fair!" complained another.

"Maybe," suggested one of the younger satraps, "we should try to find something wrong with Daniel."

The other satraps just laughed. They knew Daniel to be a loyal and righteous man, who had never done any wrong as the King's advisor.

"No, he's blameless I tell you!" one satrap shouted in frustration. "You'll never find anything wrong with Daniel, unless—" he paused deep in thought.

A sly grin came across his face. "Unless," he continued, "it has something to do with the law of his god! He'd never do anything against the god he worships."

By the end of the day, the conniving satraps came up with a wicked plan to get rid of Daniel for good. They would use the King's own pride to trick him into helping them. The next morning they presented their idea to the King.

"Sire," they said "we have all agreed you should issue a new law. Anyone who prays to any god or man other than to you in the next thirty days, shall be thrown into the lions' den. This law should be issued so that it cannot be changed. This will remind everyone in your kingdom you are a mighty and powerful king."

"I'm not sure this is such a good idea," Darius thought to himself. "But I am the most powerful king in the world. Why should people pray to anyone else?" Letting his pride get the best of him, Darius signed the law into effect that day.

Immediately the evil satraps sent spies to watch Daniel's house.

Knowing Daniel had been gone that day, a friend came to his house to tell him about the King's new law and a rumor he'd heard about the satraps' plan.

"The King wouldn't make a law like this on his own," Daniel said. "The satraps would love to have me out of their way. But I won't let the law change my actions. Everyone knows I pray to my God and I'm not going to stop now."

"But couldn't you just stop praying for the next thirty days?" his friend asked.

"Stop praying for thirty days?" said Daniel in disbelief. "That's like telling a child he can't talk to his father for a month! I pray to my Lord because I love Him. Why, I rely on Him for everything. I can't imagine going even one day without spending time with Him. The Lord controls my life and I'll gladly die for Him if necessary."

"I wish I were as brave as you," sighed his friend.

"Bravery has nothing to do with it," explained Daniel. "When you belong to the Lord you don't have to be brave. He gives you the grace to go through anything if you just trust in Him. I will honor the Lord no matter how hard it might be. Good night, my friend. Thanks for letting me know about this."

"Please be careful," begged Daniel's friend as he left and shut the door.

The new law greatly disturbed Daniel. The Babylonians did not worship the one true God and they put much pressure on Daniel to worship their gods instead. They were putting him to the greatest test yet: would Daniel continue to remain true to God even if it meant his own life?

The time had come for Daniel to pray. Taking a deep breath, Daniel opened his window, got on his knees and lifted his face and hands toward heaven.

"Oh Lord, God of Israel," Daniel prayed, "thank you for the way you have exalted me in the land of my captivity. You know how I've been faithful to follow all your laws and commands, even when it was difficult."

"Now," continued Daniel earnestly, "a law has been made that makes praying to you a crime. Oh Lord, I need your help! Please give me the grace to walk through this trial. And please help my friend understand what it means to have a personal relationship with the Living God!"

The spies watching Daniel's house were thrilled when they saw him praying. They immediately told the satraps, who came themselves to see Daniel pray the next morning.

Sure enough, at sunrise, Daniel opened his window and prayed to God, just as he did every morning.

"What our spies told us is true!" they cried in glee. "Daniel *is* praying to his god. Now we can complete our little plan!"

With their victory in sight, the satraps wasted no time in telling the King their 'good news'.

"I'm very busy," the King complained. "I hope this won't take long."

"It will only take a moment, your majesty," they said smugly. "It seems that at least one person pays no attention to your laws. We caught him praying to his god this morning, in front of an open window for all to see."

"I'll have him thrown to the lions before the sun sets today!" bellowed Darius. "Who is this lawbreaker?"

"One of the exiles from Judah," said one of the older satraps slowly. "He's your advisor, Daniel."

Darius was stunned.

"There must be some mistake," stammered the King. "Why, Daniel is my most trusted advisor—"

"There has been no mistake, your majesty," explained one of the satraps. "We saw him with our very own eyes this morning."

"But I can't possibly throw Daniel to the lions," the King groaned.

"If you don't," said the satraps firmly, "then no one throughout your kingdom will see any reason to obey any of your laws."

"I've heard enough!" yelled Darius. "Now get out! All of you!"

The King was angry at himself for agreeing to the law in the first place. He knew it was his fault Daniel was in trouble. He would do everything in his power to save his friend from the lions' den.

Darius tried to find other laws that would protect Daniel, but there were none. The satraps had been very clever and the King could find no way to rescue Daniel.

"Don't forget the law has been written so that it cannot be changed," the satraps reminded the King as sundown approached.

Darius knew he had no choice. With great sadness the King ordered his guards to bring Daniel to the palace.

Daniel's dealing with Darius' law on prayer is only one example where God's people have dealt with difficult moral decisions. Examples include Joseph (Genesis 39), Shadrach, Meshach and Abednego (Daniel 3), and Queen Esther (the book of Esther), just to name a few.

The Bible gives us many negative examples as well. Adam and Eve (Genesis 3), Jonah (the book of Jonah), and Ananias and Sapphira (Acts 5:1-11) are some of those who willfully disobeyed God and paid the consequences.

Though few of us have faced moral decisions where our lives hang in the balance, we do face small decisions of right and wrong every day. Will we lie or tell the truth, even when it's difficult? Will we do the right thing or let others pressure us into compromise?

God has given us His Word and His Holy Spirit to be our guide in these decisions. He doesn't want our conscience to degenerate into some religious list of do's and don'ts. He wants His Word to be hidden in our hearts. That Word is alive and active, judging the thoughts and attitudes of our heart. If we should sin, God is faithful to forgive us and restore a clear conscience. Then we can walk in the Light, as He is in the Light.
—Julie Voudrie (see Romans 8:1-17, Colossians 2:13-23, Ps 119:11, Hebrews 4:12 & 13, & 1 John 1:5-10)

"Daniel, I don't know what to say, " said the King sadly. "You are aware of the charges against you. Are you sure you knew about this law?"

"I must tell the truth, your majesty," replied Daniel solemnly."I knew all about the law and made the choice to disobey it. If I cannot serve God when it is difficult, then why should I serve him at all? Even if it means my life I cannot deny the One who has kept me all these years."

"You have been a loyal advisor and a close friend to me, Daniel. But you know I have no choice but to carry out the sentence against you. You've said a man's pride will destroy him, but I never thought my own pride would harm you, my dear friend."

The King paused, but he could delay his duty no longer.

"I hereby sentence you to be put into the lions' den until sunrise tomorrow," Darius commanded."May your God, whom you always serve, rescue you from the lions."

"Do not worry," replied Daniel quietly. "I am in the hands of Almighty God."

16

King Darius followed as the guards took Daniel to the lions' den. Some of the satraps followed as well to make sure the sentence against Daniel was carried out.

The sun was setting as the soldiers moved the boulder away from the den's entrance. The lions roared violently, hungry for their next meal.

But Daniel was not afraid. God had put a deep peace in his heart. Even though he did not know if he would live beyond the next few minutes, it did not matter. He had lived his life unto God and had no regrets.

"Your will be done, Lord," whispered Daniel to himself as the soldiers took him to the den's opening and dropped him through the hole. The sounds of the lions' roars became muffled as the boulder was put back in place. The entrance of the den was sealed so that no one could remove the boulder until sunrise the next day.

With great sorrow the King returned to his palace. Now that Daniel was out of their way, the satraps turned on each other. They fought over which of them should take Daniel's place.

But was Daniel *really* out of their way? Unknown to the satraps, some miraculous things had happened in the lions' den.

"Ohhhh!" said Daniel as he landed in the den on his side. He looked up to see the faces of some very hungry lions. They glared at him with ravenous eyes, licking their lips and stalking toward him with threatening growls.

Suddenly the dim room was filled with an incredibly bright light! Daniel shielded his eyes from the brilliant rays as the lions ran to hide in a corner of the den.

A voice called out from the the light: "Daniel, servant of the most High God!"

As Daniel looked back at the light, he saw the form of a beautiful angel! The angel was dressed in a robe of dazzling white and wore a sash of gold around his waist.

"Yes, I am Daniel," he said nervously, shaking in the presence of such a being.

"Do not be afraid," said the angel. "The Lord of Hosts whom you serve has found you innocent. He sent me here to save your life. Tomorrow morning you will leave this den. It will be a great witness of God's power to all the people of Babylon."

"I have shut the mouths of these lions," said the angel as he walked over to where the lions were cowering. "Now they will not be able to harm you at all. Be at peace, Daniel, servant of the most High God. The Lord has delivered you." With those words, the angel vanished just as suddenly as he had appeared.

"I can hardly believe it! Did God really send an angel to save me?" said Daniel as he looked at the lions, still hiding in the corner. Even in the fading light, he could see the lions' eyes were full of fear and none of them could open their mouths.

"This isn't a dream — it's real!" exclaimed Daniel. "The lions' mouths are shut! God has spared my life!" Daniel was overwhelmed with praise. He fell to his knees and gave thanks to God.

"O Lord, the Almighty God, You have saved me from the lions! Hallelujah! You are the all powerful and Almighty God! Bless your holy name! Thank you for sending your angel to shut the lions' mouths! May all of Babylon know that you are the one true God!"

Taking one last look at the lions still cowering in the corner, Daniel made a bed of straw for himself. He closed his eyes and fell into a peaceful sleep.

Back at the palace, however, King Darius had no peace at all. He was anxious and nervous, not knowing what was happening to Daniel in the lions' den.

"I can't eat this," said Darius as he stared blankly at the delicious meal his servants had brought him.

"Perhaps some dancing or music would make you happy," suggested one servant.

"No! There's to be no singing or dancing in the palace tonight," Darius replied. The King thought, "How can I enjoy myself knowing what I've done to my friend?"

Darius went to bed early, but he couldn't sleep. He tossed and turned all night long. "The lions are probably sleeping soundly after their big meal," King Darius groaned.

"Is there any hope for Daniel?" he wondered as the first rays of dawn appeared in the eastern sky. "Has Daniel's God been able to save him from the hungry lions? Maybe there's a chance that God has spared Daniel's life!"

The King jumped out of bed and threw on his clothes.

"Take me to the lions' den!" he ordered his driver.

The soldiers were surprised to see the King so early in the morning.

"Remove that boulder from the entrance of the den!" the King commanded the soldiers.

Darius was afraid to look down into the den, for fear of what he might see. He called out to Daniel instead.

"Daniel," cried out the King, "servant of the living God, has your God, whom you always serve, been able to rescue you from the lions?"

"O King, live forever!" answered Daniel. "My God sent his angel and has shut the mouths of the lions! They haven't even hurt me, because I was found innocent in God's eyes. Nor have I done any wrong to you, O King."

"Oh may your God be praised!" exclaimed Darius. Immediately Daniel was lifted out of the den. The mouths of the lions were released and they roared violently, angry that their meal had been denied them.

"Your God is indeed a mighty God," said King Darius. "Never in my whole life have I seen something as miraculous as this. Tonight we will celebrate with a dinner in honor of you taking charge of my kingdom. But first, I must take care of some unfinished business."

Darius summoned his satraps for yet another important announcement. The satraps had not settled their argument from the night before as to which of them was the greatest. They had even began to plot against one another in the same way they had plotted against Daniel. As the King entered the room, they hushed their arguing.

"I have chosen the one who will take charge of my kingdom," said Darius. "He is a wise and learned man and I have total trust and confidence in him. Now I would like to announce my choice: his name is *Daniel!*"

At that moment Daniel entered the room. Now it was the satraps' turn to be stunned. The bewildered satraps gasped at the sight of Daniel. They thought their little plan had worked and Daniel was out of their way for good. How could this have happened?

"But he was thrown to the lions!" exclaimed one of the older satraps. "I was there! I saw it with my own eyes!"

"Daniel was thrown into the lions' den, as you yourself witnessed," stated Darius angrily. "But God saved him. He sent an angel to shut the mouths of the lions and they didn't hurt him at all. You wicked satraps! You were trying to make Daniel look guilty while you were the guilty ones all along. Now you will be thrown to the lions yourselves! Guards, take them away!"

"We didn't mean any harm! Please don't throw us to the lions!" begged the frightened satraps. The King would not change his mind. There would be no angel to come to the satraps' rescue.

The King was so impressed by what happened to Daniel, he issued a royal decree.

"I hereby declare this proclamation be read throughout my kingdom:

'I decree that all people in my kingdom must fear and respect the God of Daniel. For the God of Daniel is the living God and his kingdom will never end. He rescues and He saves; He does great things in the heavens and on earth. The Living God has rescued Daniel from the lions' den."

People everywhere were amazed when they heard how Almighty God had saved Daniel from the lions' den. The other exiles from Judah were greatly encouraged by Daniel's deliverance. They took heart that one day God would deliver them from the Babylonians and return them to their own land in Israel.

God saved Daniel from the lions' den because he did what was right in God's sight. Daniel put his whole trust in God and did not deny the Lord, even when it meant his own life was in danger; and Daniel prospered under the reign of King Darius.

God gave Israel a land and a law and leaders, a place for them to worship and prophets to guide them. But many Israelites rejected God's gifts and his guidance. They disobeyed his law, ignored his leaders, and worshiped false gods. The prophets warned them that destruction would come if they did not return to God.

Destruction finally came with the Babylonian army. Under King Nebuchadnezzar Babylon invaded Jerusalem in 606 BC, taking Daniel and other young men to Babylon to be "retrained" as Babylonians. In 597 BC another invasion meant more exiles. Finally in 586 BC unrepentant Judah was destroyed, including the Temple. Many people died in the fighting, some fled, but thousands were taken as slaves to Babylon.

It was another fifty years before Israelites were allowed to return home. But even before God's people returned to Judah, still during the Babylonian Captivity, they returned to Him in faithful worship and prayer and the study of His law. God is our judge, holding us accountable, but he is also our redeemer, delivering us by his grace when we believe and repent and obey. —Dr. Lee Magness (see Psalm 137, Daniel 1:1-7, & 2 Chronicles 7:13 & 14)

Shepherd's Tales™ Bible Storybook Companions:

 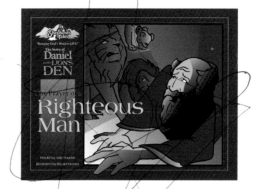

Shepherd's Tales™ Bible Story Cassettes: